FIRST COME THE ZEBRA

TO WENDY AND MARC, CASSIE AND ROSS, DINAH AND JOSH.
MANY TRIBES, ONE FAMILY.

LEE & LOW BOOKS Inc., 95 Madison Avenue, New York, NY 10016
leeandlow.com

Manufactured in China by Toppan

Book design by Tania Garcia
Book production by The Kids at Our House

The text is set in Stempel Garamond
The illustrations are rendered in ink and watercolor

(HC) 10 9 8 7 6 5 4 3 2 1
(PB) 10 9 8 7 6
First Edition

Library of Congress Cataloging-in-Publication Data
Barasch, Lynne.
First come the zebra / Lynne Barasch. — 1st ed.
        p. cm.
    Summary: When two young Kenyan boys, one Maasai and one Kikuyu, first meet, they are hostile toward each other based on traditional rivalries, but after they suddenly have to work together to save a baby in danger, the boys begin to discover what they have in common.
    Includes bibliographical references.
    ISBN 978-1-60060-365-5 (hardcover : alk. paper)   ISBN 978-1-62014-029-1 (paperback)
1. Masai (African people)—Juvenile fiction. 2. Kikuyu (African people)—Juvenile fiction. [1. Masai (African people)—Fiction. 2. Kikuyu (African people)—Fiction. 3. Cooperativeness—Fiction. 4. Kenya—Fiction.] I. Title.
PZ7.B22965Fi 2009
[E]—dc22   2008053717

FIRST COME THE ZEBRA

LYNNE BARASCH

LEE & LOW BOOKS INC. • NEW YORK

The sun is rising over the grassland in Kenya. The tall grass is lush and green after the long rainy season. Soon the great migration will begin, and nearly two million animals will come from the vast savanna in neighboring Tanzania. The grass there has been grazed down to the ground, so the animals migrate to Kenya, where there is plenty. They have done this for thousands of years.

First come the zebra. They will eat
only the very top of the grass.

Then come the wildebeest. They will eat
the middle section of the grass.

Last come the small Thomson's gazelle. They will eat
the final few inches of the grass.

Each animal will take only what it needs. By sharing the land,
there will be plenty for all. There will be peace among the grazers.

Abaani, a young Maasai boy, wakes up in the early morning. He drinks a cup of milk for breakfast and goes outside. He is ready to take the cattle out to graze for the day.

Cattle are the wealth of the Maasai. They are a source of food and money. Abaani walks alongside his family's small herd with his stick in hand.

Ahead of him Abaani sees a small roadside stall filled with fruit and vegetables from a Kikuyu farm. He has not seen this stall before today. It tells him there is a new farm nearby. A Kikuyu boy about the same age as Abaani is tending the stall.

Abaani calls out, *"Jina langu ni Abaani. Jina lako ni nani?"* My name is Abaani. Who are you?

The answer comes quickly. *"Jina langu ni Haki."* My name is Haki.

Abaani has heard the elders complain about the Kikuyu farmers. He knows that the Kikuyu farms are planted on grassland the Maasai also need for their cattle to graze. Without thinking, Abaani repeats what he has heard others say.

"You destroy our land!" Abaani shouts at Haki.

"How dare you say that to me?" answers Haki. "You sleep in a hut with your cows!"

Abaani is furious. "You crawl in the dirt!" he yells. All the while, Abaani is walking closer and closer to the stall. He raises his arm. He wishes he had a spear, not just a stick.

A group of Kamba women approaches Haki's stall. The Kamba are known for their sturdy handmade baskets called *kiondos*. The women have come to trade their baskets for some of Haki's fruit and vegetables. He turns away from Abaani to attend to business.

As the women are busy unpacking the baskets, a mother puts her baby on the ground to play. The baby is happy to be free. He wanders toward the tall grass.

"I'll distract the warthogs," Abaani calls to Haki. "You run in and get the baby."

Abaani lets out a series of screams and advances into the grass waving his stick. The warthogs turn to chase him. Haki races in and scoops up the baby in his arms.

The warthogs grunt and snort loudly as they run
after Abaani. The Kamba women hear the commotion,
and the baby's mother realizes her child is gone.

After a moment Haki appears. The mother reaches out
and takes her baby from him, a grateful smile on her face.

Then Haki grabs several pieces of firewood from under his stall and chases the warthogs, throwing the sticks as he runs. The warthogs gallop off into the bush. Abaani breathes a sigh of relief.

The baby is safe. Abaani and Haki are safe. The boys eye each other.

Haki is all right even if he is Kikuyu, Abaani thinks. But he says nothing to Haki.

Hmm. Good work, and from a Maasai, Haki thinks. But he too remains silent.

The next day, and for many days after, Abaani leads his cattle within sight of Haki's stall. Abaani is curious about the boy, but still he is reluctant to speak to Haki.

Haki is curious too, and he begins to look forward to seeing Abaani and his cattle nearby. Finally one day, Haki waves.

Abaani walks a little closer. Then, cautiously, he waves back.

Soon an idea begins to take shape.

"What if I give you some of our fruit and vegetables in exchange for some of your cows' milk?" says Haki.

Abaani thinks for a few moments. "We could try it," he says. "It would really surprise everyone in my family."

"We will share what we have," Haki adds.

"Yes, we should try it," agrees Abaani. "And maybe our families will become friends too, just like we have."

As the sun sinks in the sky, Abaani and Haki hear the sound of distant hoofbeats. They look toward the horizon. The great migration is beginning. The zebra, the wildebeest, and the gazelle will once again share the grassland. Soon, the boys hope, the Maasai and the Kikuyu will find their own peaceful way to share the land.

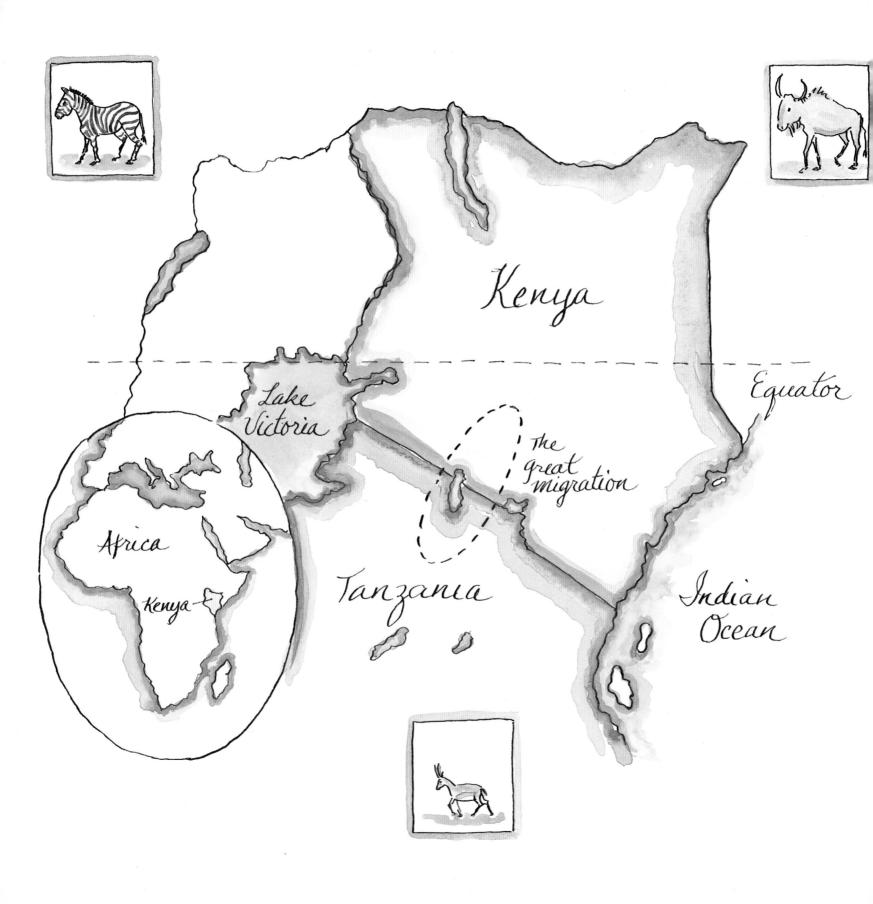

Author's Note

In 2007, my family and I visited Kenya. The idea for this story came from long conversations with our guides during that trip.

To be in Kenya today is to see twenty-first century life clash with a way of life that hasn't changed very much in hundreds of years. The steel and glass towers of Nairobi, the capital, are a long way from the stick and dung huts of rural villages. Throughout the country, many such sharp contrasts in economic and social conditions are evident.

Of the peoples living in Kenya, the Kikuyu, who are traditionally farmers, are the majority. The Maasai, a smaller, seminomadic group, are cattle herders. The conflicts between the Maasai and the Kikuyu are deep-seated and ongoing. Over the years the Maasai have lost much of their grazing grassland, which has been taken over for farms worked by the Kikuyu. This and the problem of grazing cattle straying between grassland and farmland continue to cause clashes and protests.

Recently, however, attitudes have begun to change. The youth of the country have become the hope for the future. Especially among the young, attitudes and opinions about strong group loyalty are undergoing a slow but steady transformation. People are coming together and learning to coexist peacefully.

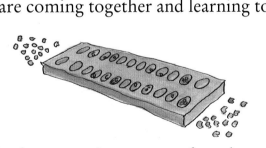

The boys in this story play an ancient game referred to as *mancala*. Mancala is a type of board game that has several names and local variations, depending on where in the world it is being played. To play, small pieces, usually pebbles or stones, are put into shallow pits carved in a board or dug out of the ground. Two players compete by moving pieces from one pit to another. The object is to capture as many pieces as possible before one of the players clears his or her side of all pieces. The player with the most pieces at the end of the game wins.

Pronunciation Guide and Glossary

Abaani (ah-BAH-nee): name meaning "someone who heals animals and people"

gazelle (guh-ZEL): small African and Asian antelope

Haki (hah-KEE): name meaning "justice"

Jina lako ni nani? (JEE-nah LAH-koh nee NAH-nee): Who are you? What is your name?

Jina langu ni . . . (JEE-nah lahn-GOO nee): My name is . . .

Kamba (KAHM-buh): member of a people of central Kenya

Kenya (KEN-yuh): country in East Africa

Kikuyu (kee-KOO-yoo): member of a people of central and southern Kenya

kiondo (kee-ON-doh): handwoven basket traditionally made by the Kamba and Kikuyu of Kenya

Maasai (mah-SIGH *or* MAH-sigh): member of a people of Kenya and parts of Tanzania

mancala (myn-CAH-lah): board game with rows of pits in which game pieces are placed; also spelled *mankala*

migrate (MY-grayt): to move from one place or region to another

migration (my-GRAY-shun): process or act of migrating

savanna (suh-VAH-nuh): grassland with scattered trees

Tanzania (tan-zuh-NEE-uh): country in East Africa

warthog (WORT-hog *or* WORT-hawg): wild African hog

wildebeest (WIL-duh-beast): large African antelope

zebra (ZEE-bruh): African mammal related to the horse but with dark and light stripes

Acknowledgments

Thank you to the following people for their advice and guidance during the preparation of this book: Henry W. Art, PhD, Professor of Biology, Williams College; Donna Barkman, children's literature specialist; Ashley Bryan, children's book author and illustrator; Barbara Jones, children's librarian in Kenya, and her colleague Liz Atieno; Joan Kindig, EdD, Associate Professor, Department of Early, Elementary, and Reading Education, James Madison University; Effie Lee Morris, former children's services librarian and Coordinator of Children's Services of the San Francisco Library; Gaby Nyausi, educator in Kenya; and Ramenga Mtaali Osotsi, PhD, Professor, Department of English, James Madison University.

Author's Sources

Some of the research for this book comes from the author's primary observations while in Kenya as well as from conversations with guides and local experts there.

Mancala boards vary in the number of pits per side. The images of the mancala board in this book are based on boards the author saw being used in Kenya.

ACF: African Conservation Foundation, www.africanconservation.org

Adamson, Joy. *The Peoples of Kenya*. London: Collins and Harvill Press, 1973.

BBC News. "Tribalism 'rampant' in Kenyan workplace," January 18, 2006, news.bbc.co.uk/2/hi/africa/4624698.stm

Blauer, Ettagale. "Mystique of the Masai." *The World and I*, March 1987, 497–513.

Maasai Association. "Maasai Issues in Summary," www.maasai-association.org/opinion.html

Payne, Doris L. "Maa Language Project." University of Oregon, www.uoregon.edu/~maasai/

Rule, Sheila. "Oloitokitok Journal; The Lionhearted Masai: Besieged by Modern Life." *New York Times*, March 28, 1988.

Saitoti, Tepilit Ole. *The Worlds of a Maasai Warrior: An Autobiography*. Berkeley and Los Angeles: University of California Press, 1988.

The Game of Bao, or Mancala, in East Africa. "Michezo ya Mbao—Mankala in East Africa," www.driedger.ca/mankala/Man-1.html

The Online Guide to Traditional Games. "Mancala, Oware and Bao," www.tradgames.org.uk/games/Mancala.htm

UNHCR/Refworld. "Assessment for Maasai in Kenya," December 31, 2003, www.unhcr.org/refworld/topic,463af2212,469f2e502,469f3aa666,0.html

U.S. Department of State, Bureau of African Affairs. "Kenya Facts at a Glance," 2004.

Wainaina, Binyavanga. "No Country for Old Hatreds." *New York Times*, January 6, 2008.

Wax, Emily. "Growing Beyond the Pull of the Tribe in Kenya: Nairobi Teenagers Find New Unity in Contemporary Culture, Even as Old Ties Persist." *Washington Post*, September 18, 2005.